CW01162907

LETTERS
NUMBERS
COLOURS

Heather Amery, Judy Hindley
and Angela Wilkes

Illustrated by Colin King

Consultant: Betty Root

Aa

Angry alligators chop apples with axes

Bb

Bad baby bears peel bananas in bed

Cc

Cowboy cat rides a camel with a cap

Dd

Dusty donkeys dance with dirty dogs

Ee

Enormous elephants smash eleven eggs

Ff

Four fuzzy foxes eat funny fish

Gg

Guzzling goats chew gaps in garden gates.

Hh

Happy hippos live in huge hen houses

Ii

Itchy imps sleep inside igloos

Jj

Jolly jaguars jump over juicy jellies

Kk

Kind kangaroos fly kites for kittens

Ll

Lazy little lions juggle with lumpy lemons

Mm

Monsters play with monkeys on the moon

Nn

Nine nurses nibble nuts in a nest

Oo

Odd ostriches often kick oranges

Pp

Pink pigs swim in a pool with pandas

Qq

Quiet queens ask quick questions

Rr

Red rabbits romp with rhinos in the rain

Ss

Seven silly soldiers fall off a seesaw

Tt

Ten toy tigers watch television in a tent

Uu

Ugly uncles hold umbrellas upside down

Vv

Violins and vases look very silly in vests

Ww

Wet wolves watch a witch in a wood

Xx

Six foxes play xylophones in boxes

Yy

Yawning monkeys eat yellow yogurt

Zz

Zebras with zips live in zoos

Look for the letters

a panda
b cabbage
c pelican
d bed
e hen
f giraffe
g tiger
h hedgehog
i fish
j banjo
k monkey
l umbrella

m lemon	n banana	o dog
p hippo	q aquarium	r kangaroo
s seesaw	t kitten	u duck
		v television
w sandwich	x axe	y yoyo
		z lizard

Find the letters

A B C D E F G H I J K L M

N O P Q R S T U V W X Y Z

Now trace and colour the letters

Aa Bb Cc Dd Ee
Ff Gg Hh Ii Jj Kk
Ll Mm Nn Oo Pp
Qq Rr Ss Tt Uu
Vv Ww Xx Yy Zz

NUMBERS

The story of a cake

1 one ★

One cook made a cake.

4 four ★★ ★★

Four rhinos caught it.

5 five ★★ ★★ ★

Five clowns pulled off the cake.

6 six ✦✦ ✦✦ ✦✦

Six acrobats picked it up.

7 seven

Seven crocodiles snapped at the cake.

8 eight ✶✶ ✶✶ ✶✶ ✶✶

Eight firemen saved it.

9 nine

Nine bees buzzed round the cake.

10 ten ★★ ★★ ★★ ★★ ★★

Ten ducks splashed it.

11 eleven

Eleven fish swam under the cake.

12 twelve ✶✶ ✶✶ ✶✶ ✶✶ ✶✶ ✶✶

Twelve frogs jumped over it.

★★

13 thirteen

Thirteen butterflies flew off with the cake

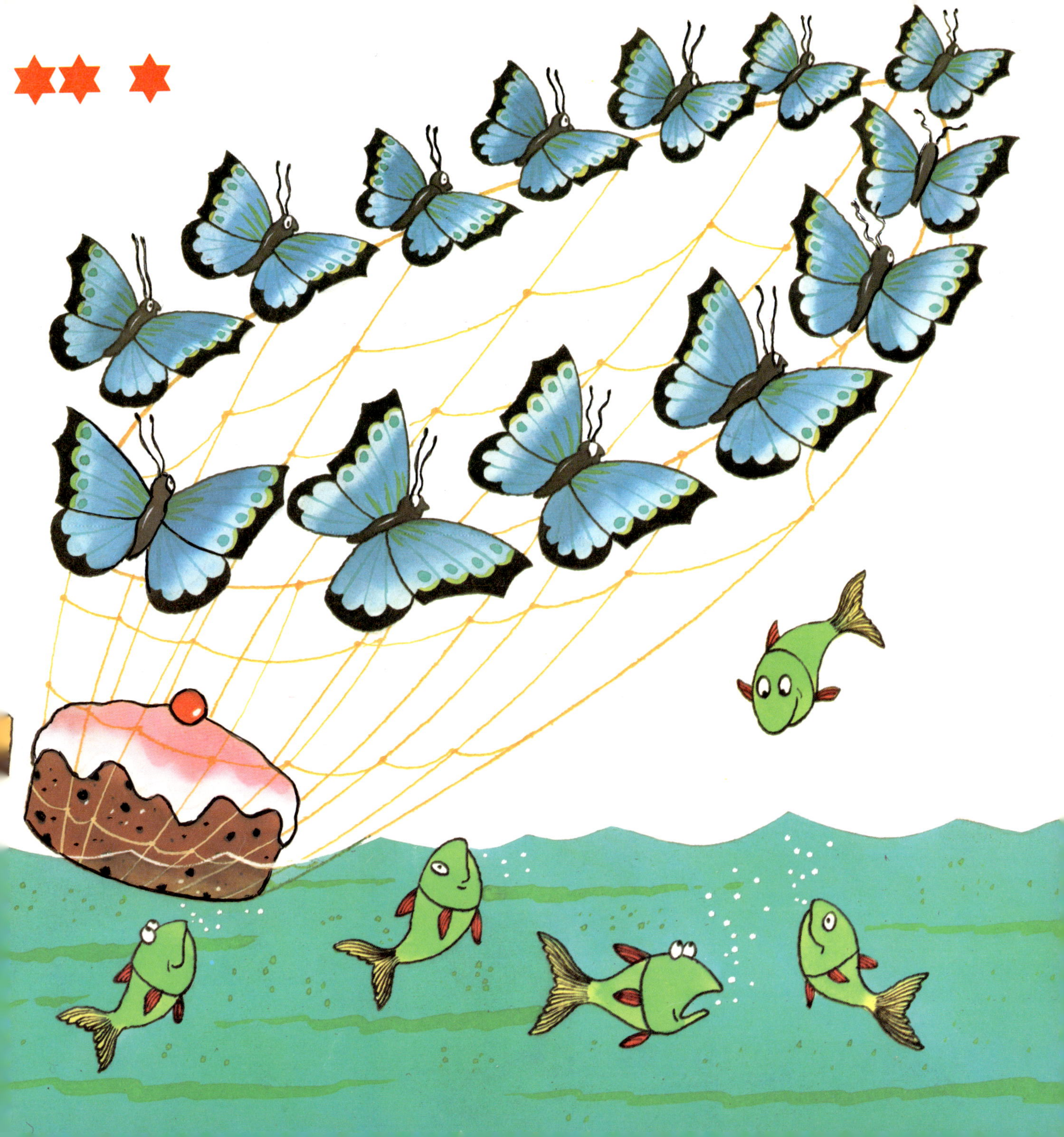

14 fourteen ✶✶ ✶✶ ✶✶ ✶✶ ✶✶ ✶✶ ✶✶

Fourteen soldiers shot at it.

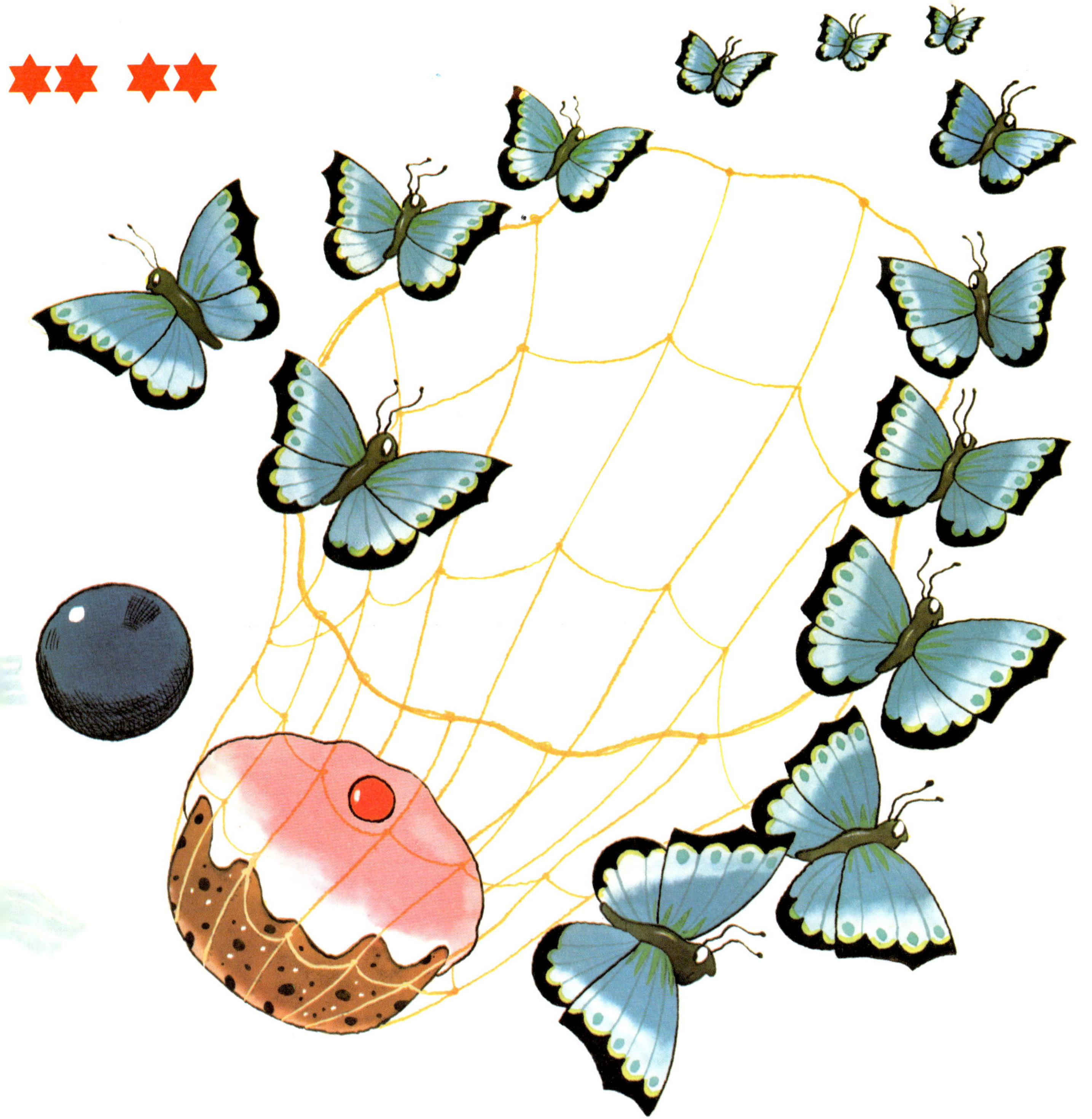

15 fifteen

Fifteen owls tried to peck the cake.

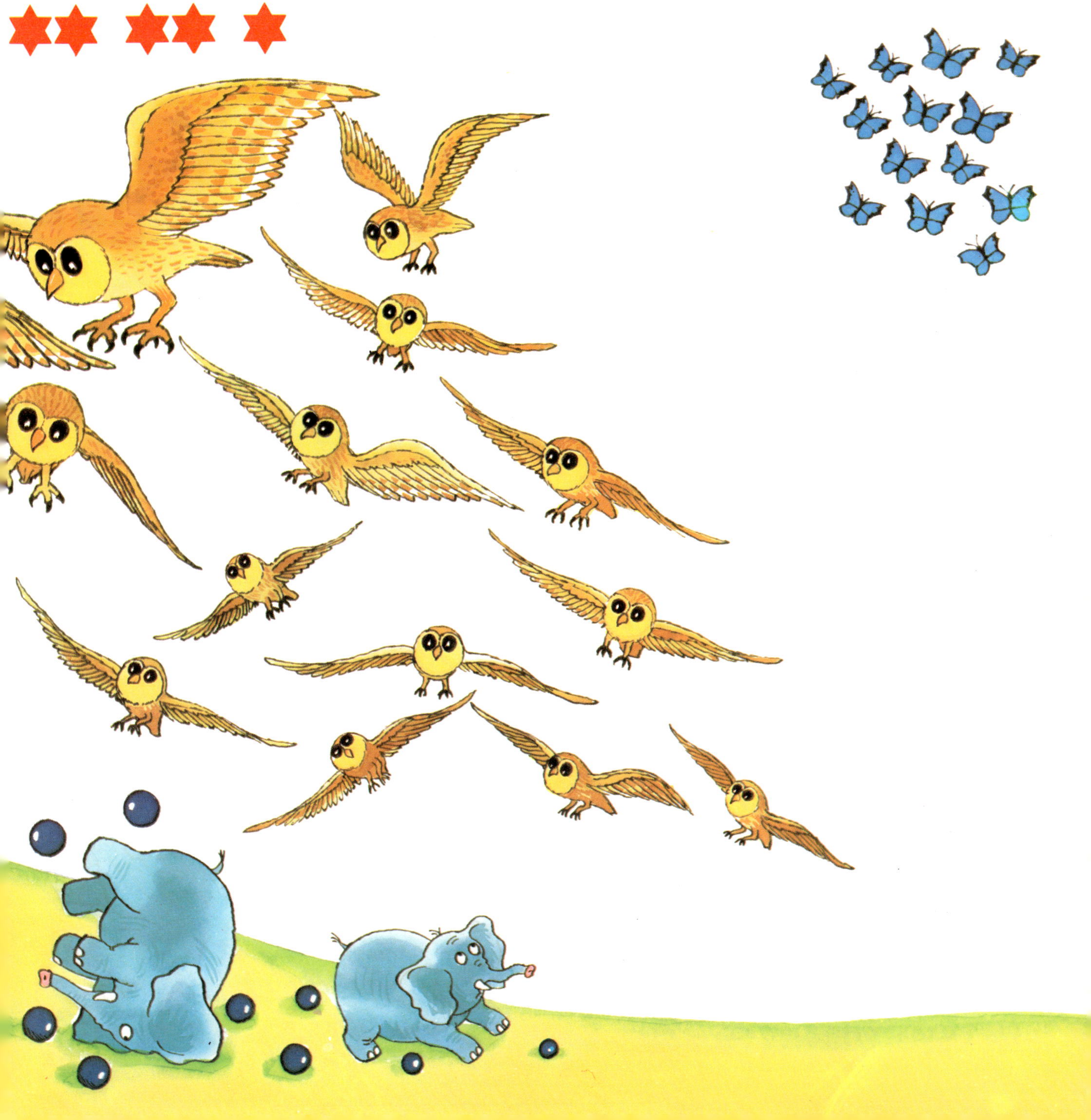

16 sixteen

Sixteen bears ran to catch it.

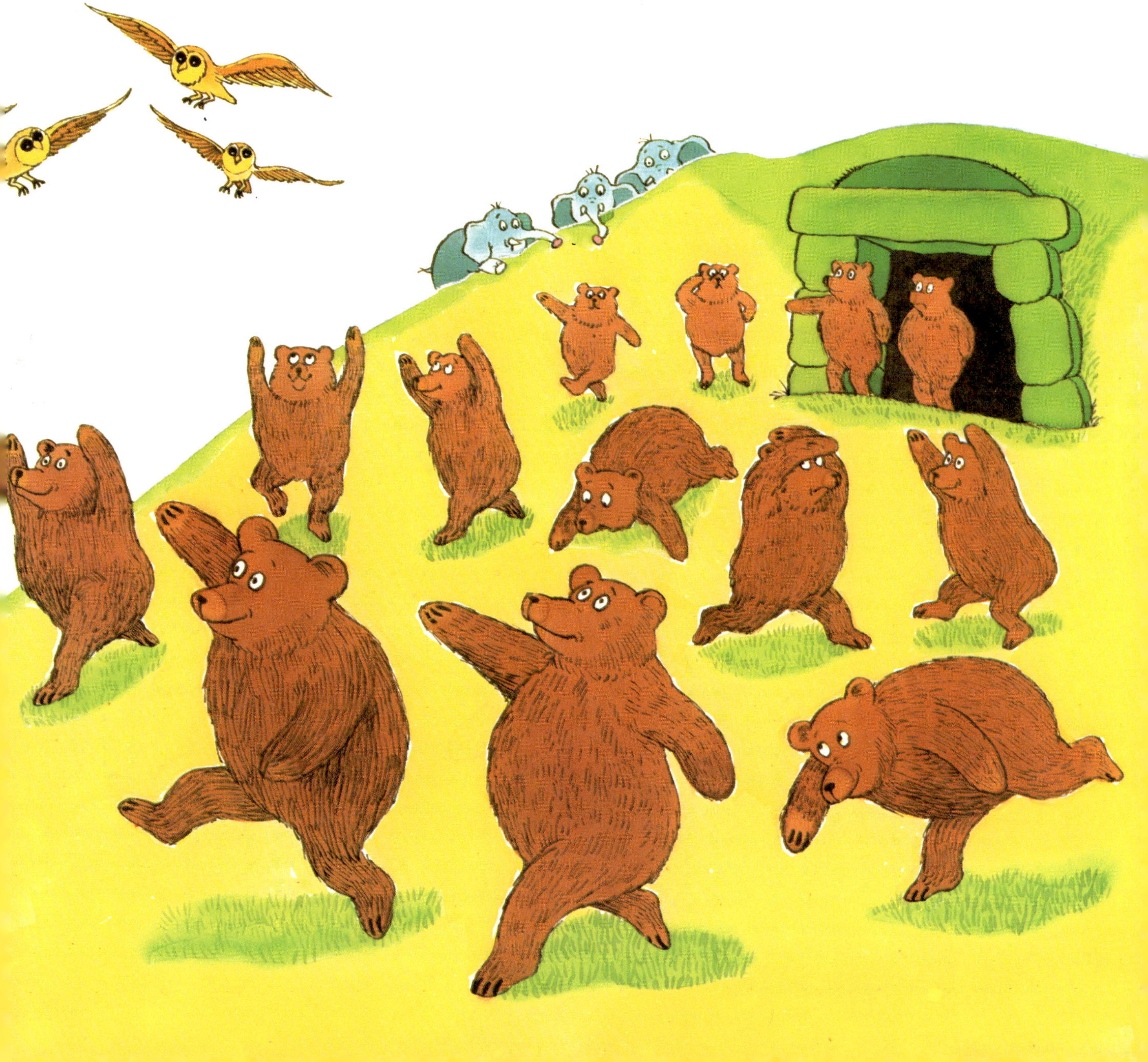

17 seventeen ✶✶ ✶✶ ✶✶ ✶✶ ✶✶

Seventeen squirrels tied up the cake.

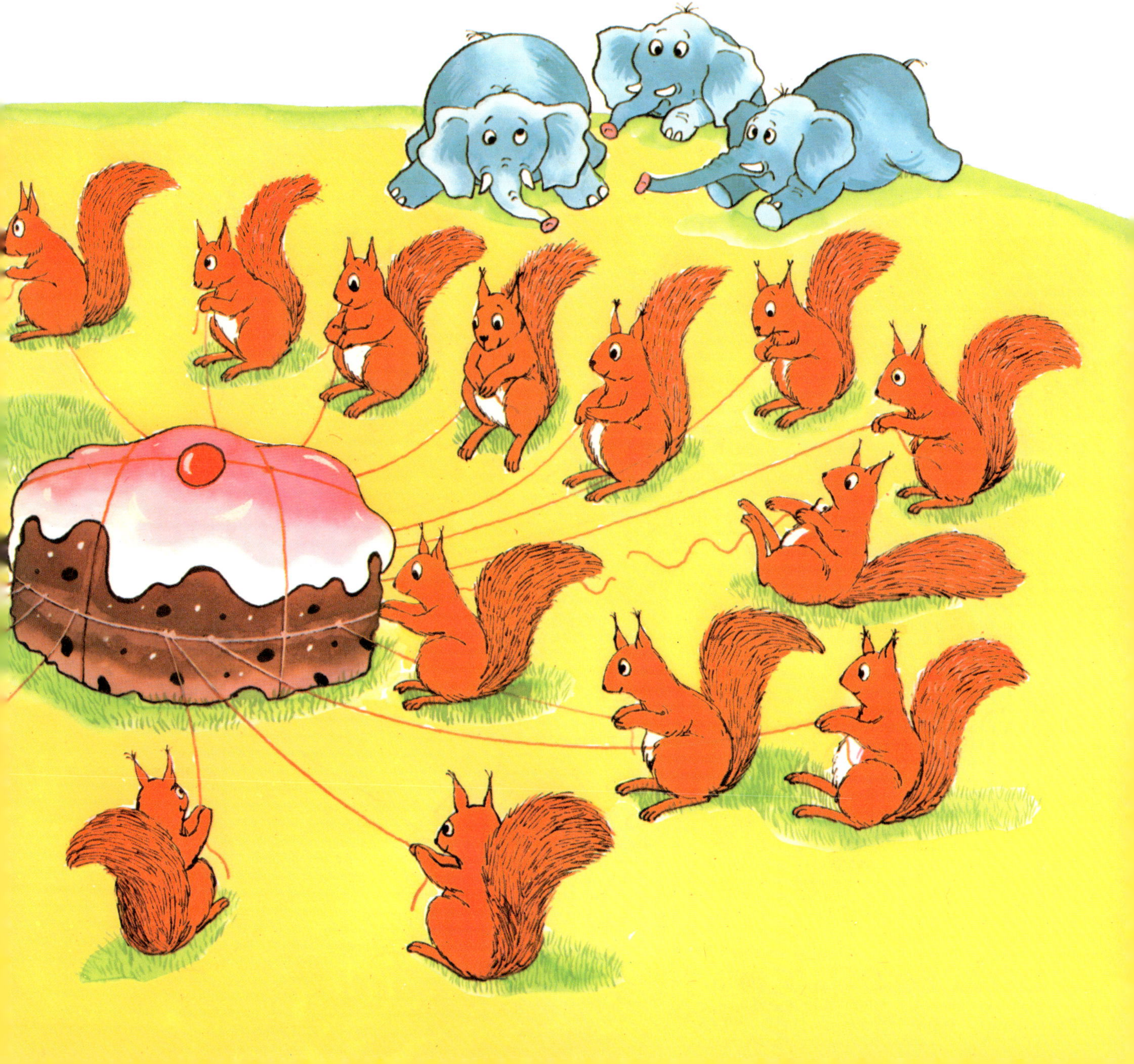

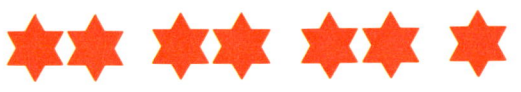

18 eighteen

Eighteen mice tried to ride on it.

✶✶ ✶✶ ✶✶ ✶✶

19 nineteen ✶✶ ✶✶ ✶✶ ✶✶ ✶✶ ✶✶

Nineteen tortoises marched along with th

ake.

20 twenty ✶✶ ✶✶ ✶✶ ✶✶ ✶✶

Twenty children ate it.

And only the crumbs were left.

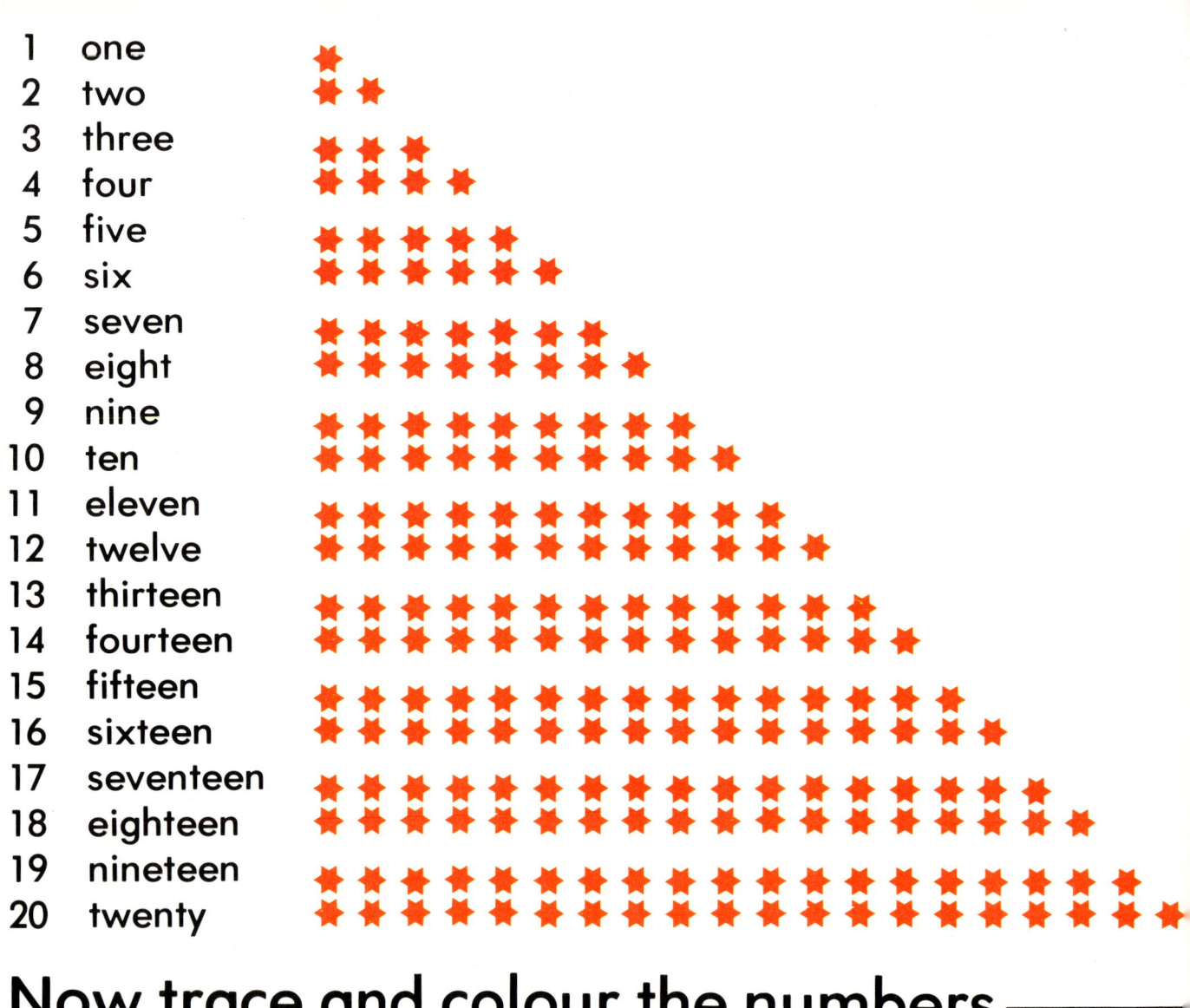

1	one
2	two
3	three
4	four
5	five
6	six
7	seven
8	eight
9	nine
10	ten
11	eleven
12	twelve
13	thirteen
14	fourteen
15	fifteen
16	sixteen
17	seventeen
18	eighteen
19	nineteen
20	twenty

Now trace and colour the numbers

1 2 3 4 5 6 7 8 9 10
11 12 13 14 15 16 17 18 19 20

COLOURS

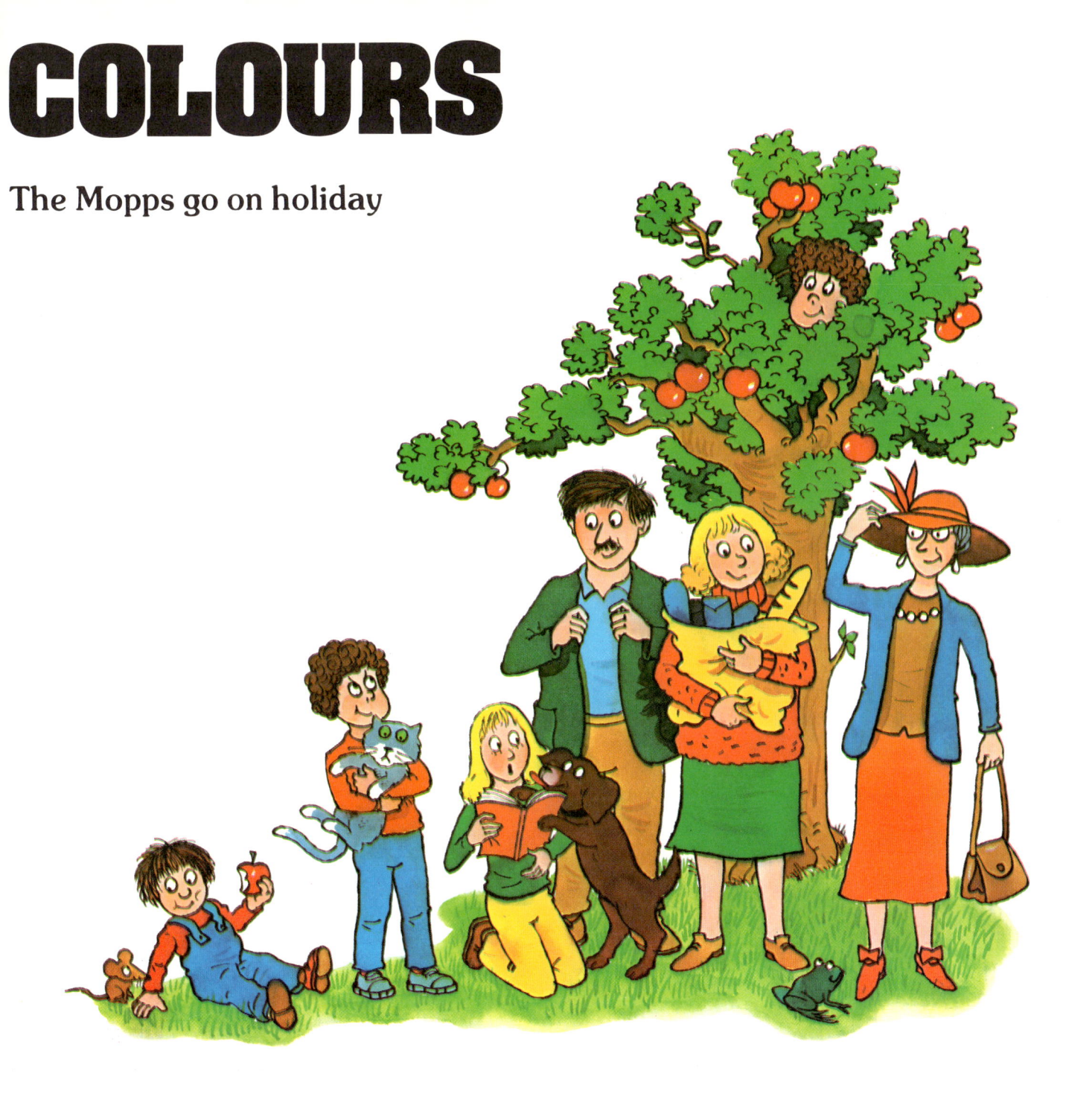

The Mopps go on holiday

orange

The Mopps are going to a farm.

Mr. Mopp is having trouble with the car.

blue

The Mopps have a picnic by the sea.

They laugh at the people on the boat.

yellow

At the farm the hay has been cut.

The Mopps load it on to the cart.

green

Then they pick the apples.

Mr. Mopp must be more careful.

brown

Baby Mopp has left a gate open.

The cows have escaped from their field.

white

And the sheep have got into the garden

Look at them playing with the washing.

black

The farmer takes the Mopps riding.

They are trying to stay on their horses.

purple

The farmer drives his truck to market.

The Mopps help to unload the plums.

grey

On the way back they see a parade.

The circus is coming to town.

red

Then they see some firemen.

They are pretending to put out a fire.

pink

In the evening it is bath time.

What a mess the Mopps are making.

At last the Mopps have gone to sleep.
What are they dreaming about?

Look on the next page as well.

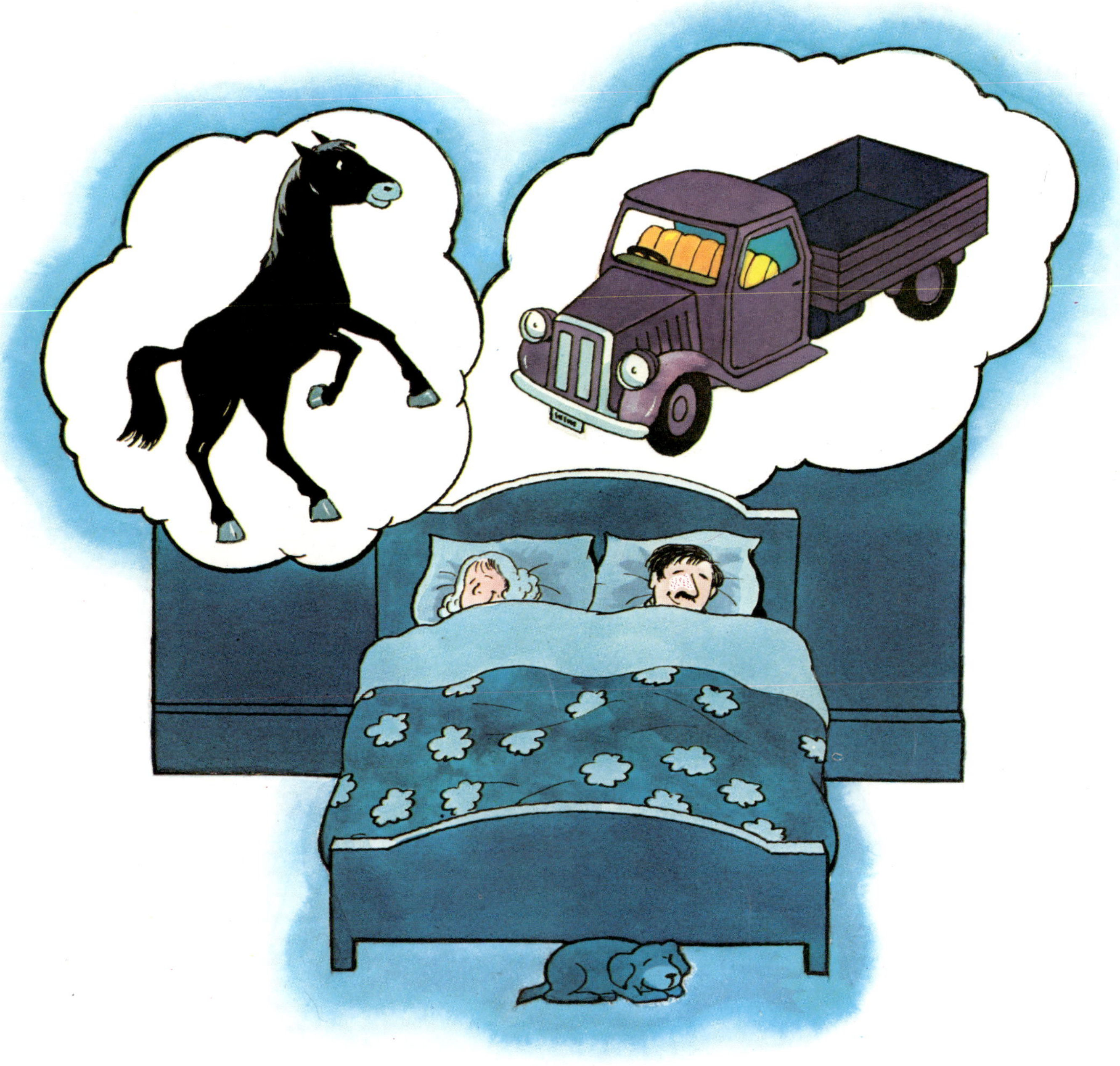

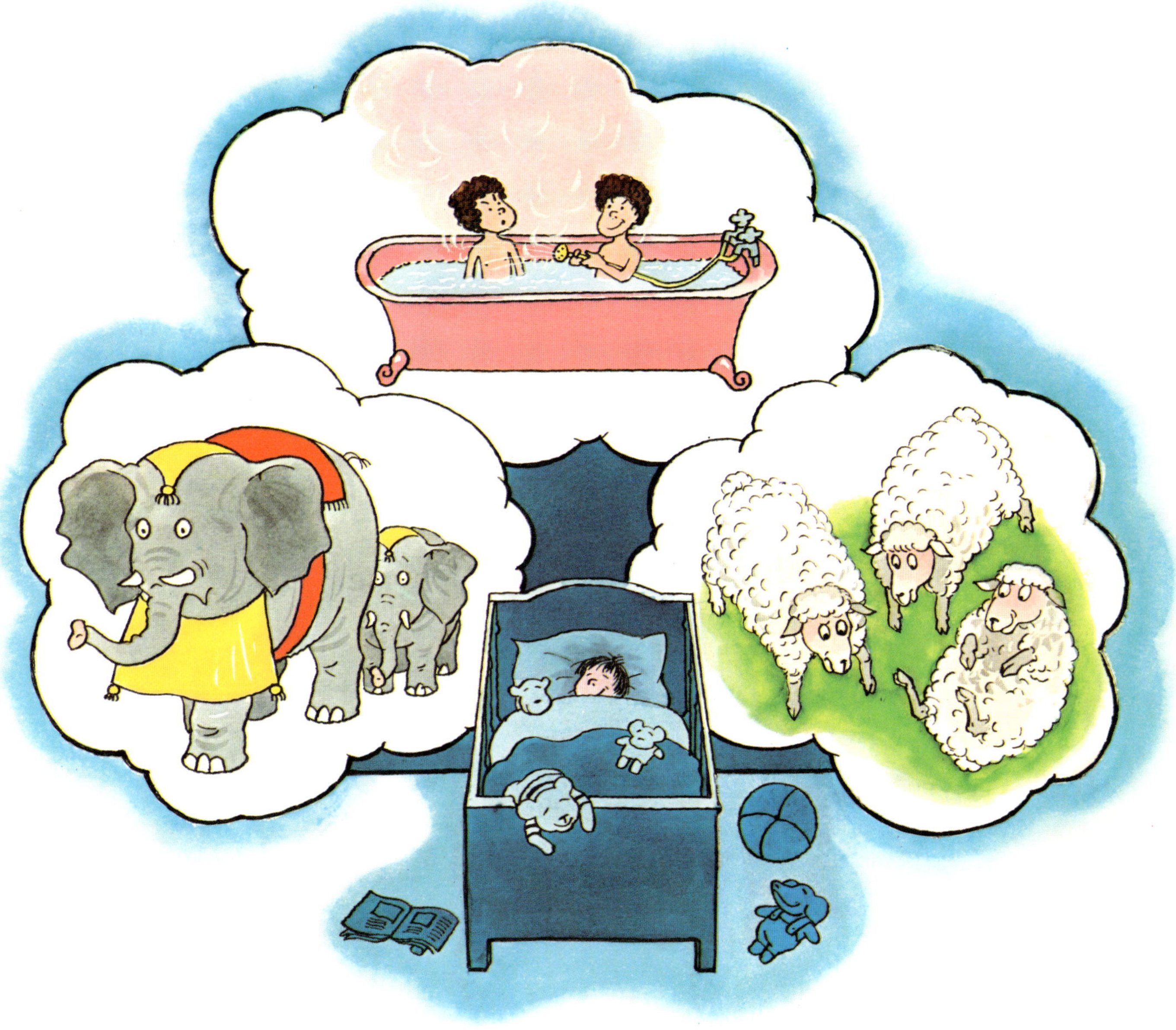

The Mopps in the rain.

Can you find the yellow umbrellas?

The Mopps have put on their coats.

Find the boots, gloves, hat and scarf to match the colour of their coats.

Puzzle Pictures

Look at these two pictures.

Which things have changed colour?

Now trace and colour the flowers

orange
red
blue
yellow
green
brown
black
purple
pink
grey

First published in 1979
by Usborne Publishing Ltd.
20 Garrick Street,
London WC2 9BJ, England
© Usborne Publishing Ltd 1979

Printed in Belgium

All rights reserved. No part of this publication may be reproduced, stored in a retrieval system or transmitted in any form or by any means, electronic, mechanical, photocopying, recording or otherwise, without the prior permission of the publisher.